HANDICAP INTERNATIONAL

In some parts of the world children can be carefree and happy-go-lucky. In other parts of the world, mutilation and death are close by, hidden underground or in toys or in little yellow bottles.

For many children, life can be forever changed in the blink of an eye. A game can become a terrible nightmare and leave a child badly disabled. Every day, Handicap International sees the consequences for children and their families. Handicap International is dedicated to fighting for a more just and welcoming world, a world without landmines, without cluster munitions, where all children have a place in spite of their origins, history, or disability.

In more than sixty countries, Handicap International helps and supports people with disabilities to improve their self-reliance, regain their independence, and claim their place in society.

Co-recipient of the 1997 Nobel Peace Prize for its fight against anti-personnel mines.

Claire Fehrenbach
Executive Director
Handicap International • Canada

The Little Yellow Bottle

written by
Angèle Delaunois

illustrated by
Christine Delezenne

Second Story Press

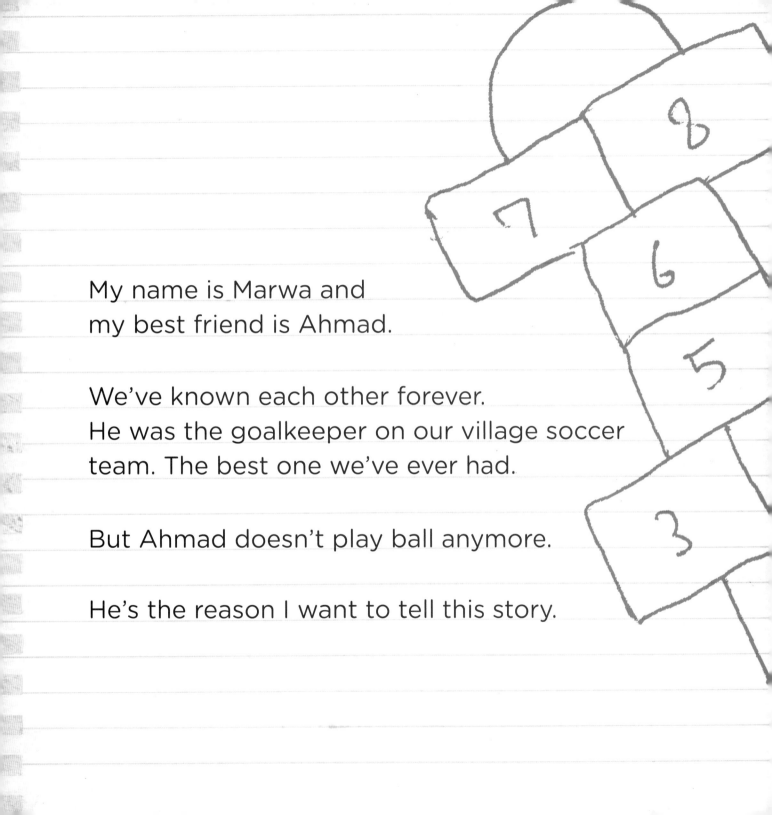

My name is Marwa and
my best friend is Ahmad.

We've known each other forever.
He was the goalkeeper on our village soccer
team. The best one we've ever had.

But Ahmad doesn't play ball anymore.

He's the reason I want to tell this story.

Ahmad

Not long ago, my country was at war. In our village, we knew that fighting was going on. We saw smoke and we heard explosions, but we believed all that was far away.

We were mostly thinking of the harvest we had to help bring in, the fruit that was ripe enough to pick, the animals we had to tend — and soccer, soccer, soccer! We just loved to play. We weren't at war with anyone.

But one day, like a cloud of angry wasps,
airplanes flew over our houses.

They spewed out
a string of big gray
objects that fell on the
countryside near our village.

They were bombs,
someone said. We heard a few
explosions, then an eerie silence fell.
No birds sang.

At first, we were terrified. We held our breath.
And then, after a few days, as all children do,
we forgot a little.

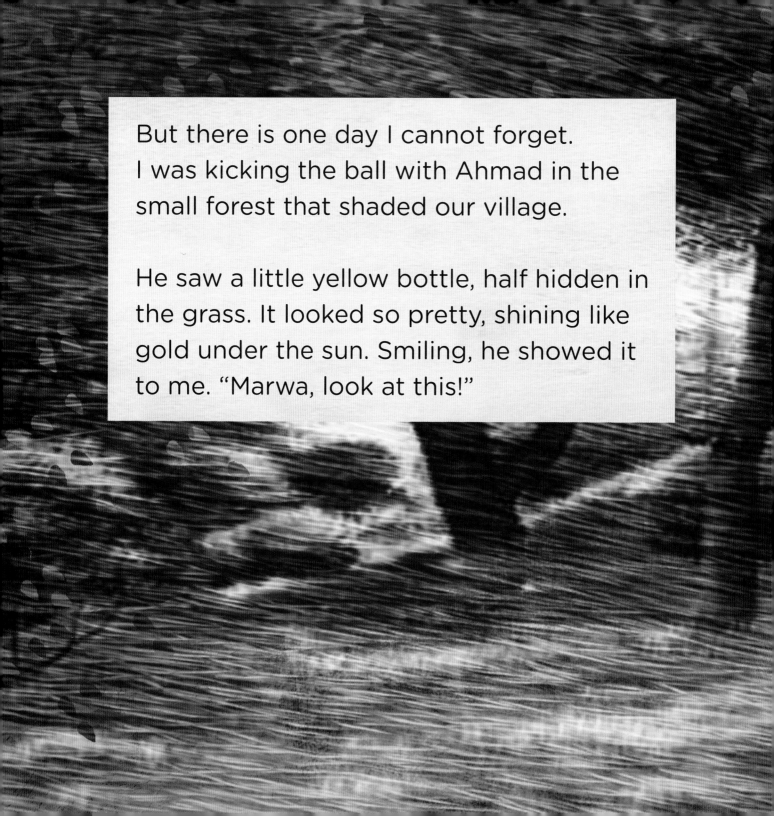

But there is one day I cannot forget.
I was kicking the ball with Ahmad in the
small forest that shaded our village.

He saw a little yellow bottle, half hidden in
the grass. It looked so pretty, shining like
gold under the sun. Smiling, he showed it
to me. "Marwa, look at this!"

I saw the yellow bottle in his hand, but I didn't have time to say a word. An intense light blinded us. Pain shot through my body as if a thousand fires were burning me all at the same time. I heard Ahmad fall to the ground, screaming.

Then, everything went black.

When I came to, I couldn't see. I hurt all over and I was really scared. I don't know how long I was in the dark. Slowly, little by little, light started to creep in.

At first, I saw everything through a mist, with hazy colors. Then I started to recognize people and objects around me.

And finally, I found my eyes.

My body was covered in bandages.

That little yellow bottle was inside
the gray bombs that the planes had
dropped all over our countryside.
When Ahmad picked it up, the bottle
exploded and sent thousands of
small pieces, as sharp as razor blades,
through the air. My face, chest, and
arms were pierced by these slivers.

The doctor caring for me promised
that I would heal.

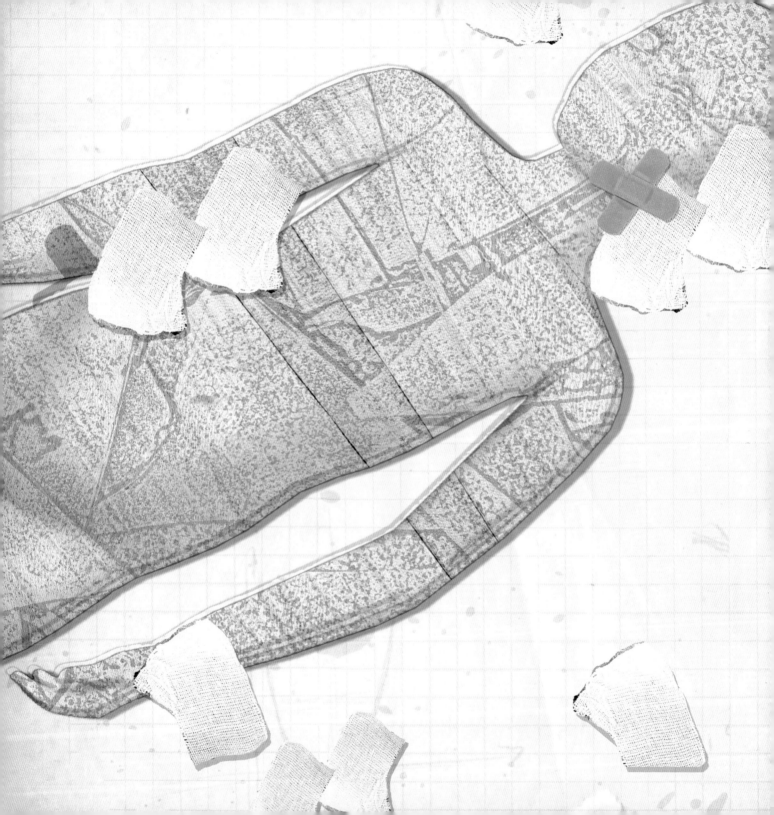

It was much worse for Ahmad.

Even the best doctors in the world couldn't help him. They had to amputate his hand and his leg. For days, my friend hovered between life and death. I think he was afraid to come back to us.

Then, he woke up. When he realized he would never walk or run like before, Ahmad turned and faced the wall. He didn't talk. He forgot how to smile.

Then one day Ahmad had a special visitor.

It was someone who also had met with a yellow bottle. We could hardly tell that it was an artificial leg under his trousers. He couldn't play soccer any more, but he could walk, drive a car, climb stairs, and even run in his own way.

He had laughing eyes and joked around with us.

He stayed with Ahmad for a long time.
He told him of his pain, his sorrow, his anger.

He also taught Ahmad that having hope and living life to the fullest are more powerful than those yellow bottles.

Thanks to his new friend, Ahmad realized that he could still do a lot of little things — and even big things.

My friend started to talk and to smile and to live again. He learned to walk with crutches.

Later, he learned to walk with a new leg.
At first, everything was so painful
that he thought he would
never succeed.

But Ahmad is super strong, and he persisted. Now, he walks just like everyone else...well, almost.

Ahmad no longer plays goalkeeper on the soccer field in our village, but he has become the best coach we've ever had.

I'm really proud of him.

My name is Marwa. I'm telling this story to honor the courage of Ahmad and all the children in the world like him. I hope you won't forget them.

Library and Archives Canada Cataloguing in Publication

Delaunois, Angèle
[Petite bouteille jaune. English]

The little yellow bottle / by Angèle Delaunois ;
illustrated by Christine Delezenne.

Translation of: Une petite bouteille jaune.

ISBN 978-1-926920-34-4

I. Delezenne, Christine II. Title. III. Title: Petite bouteille jaune. English.

PS8557.E433P4713 2011   jC843'.54   C2011-903275-9

Second Story Press gratefully acknowledges the support of the Ontario Arts Council
and the Canada Council for the Arts for our publishing program. We acknowledge
the financial support of the Government of Canada through the Book Publishing
Industry Development Program.

Printed and bound in China

ONTARIO ARTS COUNCIL
CONSEIL DES ARTS DE L'ONTARIO

Canada Council   Conseil des Arts
for the Arts   du Canada

Published by
SECOND STORY PRESS
20 Maud Street, Suite 401
Toronto, Ontario, Canada
M5V 2M5
www.secondstorypress.ca